by Michael Sandler

Consultants: Colin Jose, Historian, National Soccer Hall of Fame, Oneonta, NY
Jack Huckel, Director of Communications, National Soccer Hall of Fame, Oneonta, NY

New York, New York

Credits

Editorial development by Judy Nayer

Cover and title page, STAFF/AFP/Getty Images; Page 4-5 (both), From the archives of the National Soccer Hall of Fame, Oneonta, NY; 6, Kenneth Batelman; 7, ©Jeff Goldberg/Danita Delimont–Agent; 8, Popperfoto.com; 9, Joe LeMonnier; 10, ©Bettmann/CORBIS; 11, Popperfoto.com; 12, Courtesy of the Catholic Youth Council —St. Louis, Mo.; 13, Lawrence Migdale / Photo Researchers, Inc.; 14, ©Bettmann/CORBIS; 15, AP/Wide World Photos; 16, AP/Wide World Photos; 17, Keystone/Getty Images; 18, From the archives of the National Soccer Hall of Fame, Oneonta, NY; 19, Keystone/Getty Images; 20-27 (all 8 photos), From the archives of the National Soccer Hall of Fame, Oneonta, NY; 28, Jim Bourg/Getty Images.

Design and production by
Ralph Cosentino

Library of Congress Cataloging-in-Publication Data

Sandler, Michael.
  Soccer : the amazing U.S. World Cup team / by Michael Sandler.
    p. cm. — (Upsets & comebacks)
  Includes bibliographical references and index.
  ISBN 1-59716-169-1 (library binding) — ISBN 1-59716-195-0 (pbk.)
  1. Soccer—United States—Juvenile literature. 2. Soccer teams—United States—Juvenile literature. 3. World Cup (Soccer) (1950)—Juvenile literature. I. Title. II. Series.

GV943.25.S26 2006
796.3340973—dc22

2005026086

Copyright ©2006 Bearport Publishing Company, Inc. All rights reserved. No part of this publication may be reproduced in whole or in part, stored in a retrieval system, or transmitted in any form or by any means, electronic, mechanical, photocopying, recording, or otherwise, without written permission from the publisher.

For more information, write to Bearport Publishing Company, Inc., 101 Fifth Avenue, Suite 6R, New York, New York 10003. Printed in the United States of America.

1 2 3 4 5 6 7 8 9 10

Codman Sq. Branch Library
690 Washington Street
Dorchester, MA 02124-3511

JAN - - 2007

Table of Contents

Hopeless?..4
The Game of Soccer....................................6
The World Cup..8
England's Team..10
Soccer in America....................................12
America's Team..14
Brazil..16
The Big Game..18
Hanging Tough..20
Heads Up!..22
Holding the Lead....................................24
The Little Team That Could....................26

Just the Facts..28
History of the World Cup........................29
Glossary..30
Bibliography..31
Read More..31
Learn More Online..................................31
Index..32
About the Author....................................32

Hopeless?

The U.S. soccer players had traveled thousands of miles from home. They stood on a strange field in a faraway land. They were about to play England, the best team in the world. No one thought the U.S. team had a chance. Everyone expected them to lose.

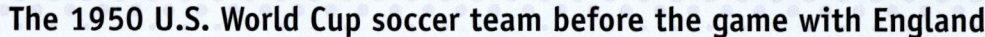

The 1950 U.S. World Cup soccer team before the game with England

Walter Bahr

The **stadium** was packed with eager fans. Few, however, thought the game would even be close. After all, the English were the "Kings of Soccer."

Yet midway through the first half, the game was still tied. Neither team had scored. Then, U.S. player Walter Bahr (BAR) kicked the ball toward England's **goal**. It sailed into the air.

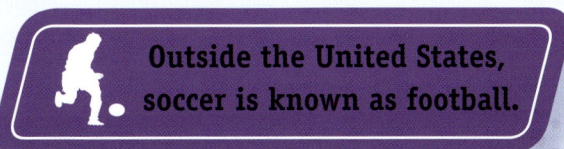

Outside the United States, soccer is known as football.

The Game of Soccer

Soccer is a simple game. Players try to score goals by sending a ball into a rectangular net.

To control the ball, players mainly use their feet. They "dribble" the ball, moving it while running. They pass the ball to teammates. They kick it hard across the field.

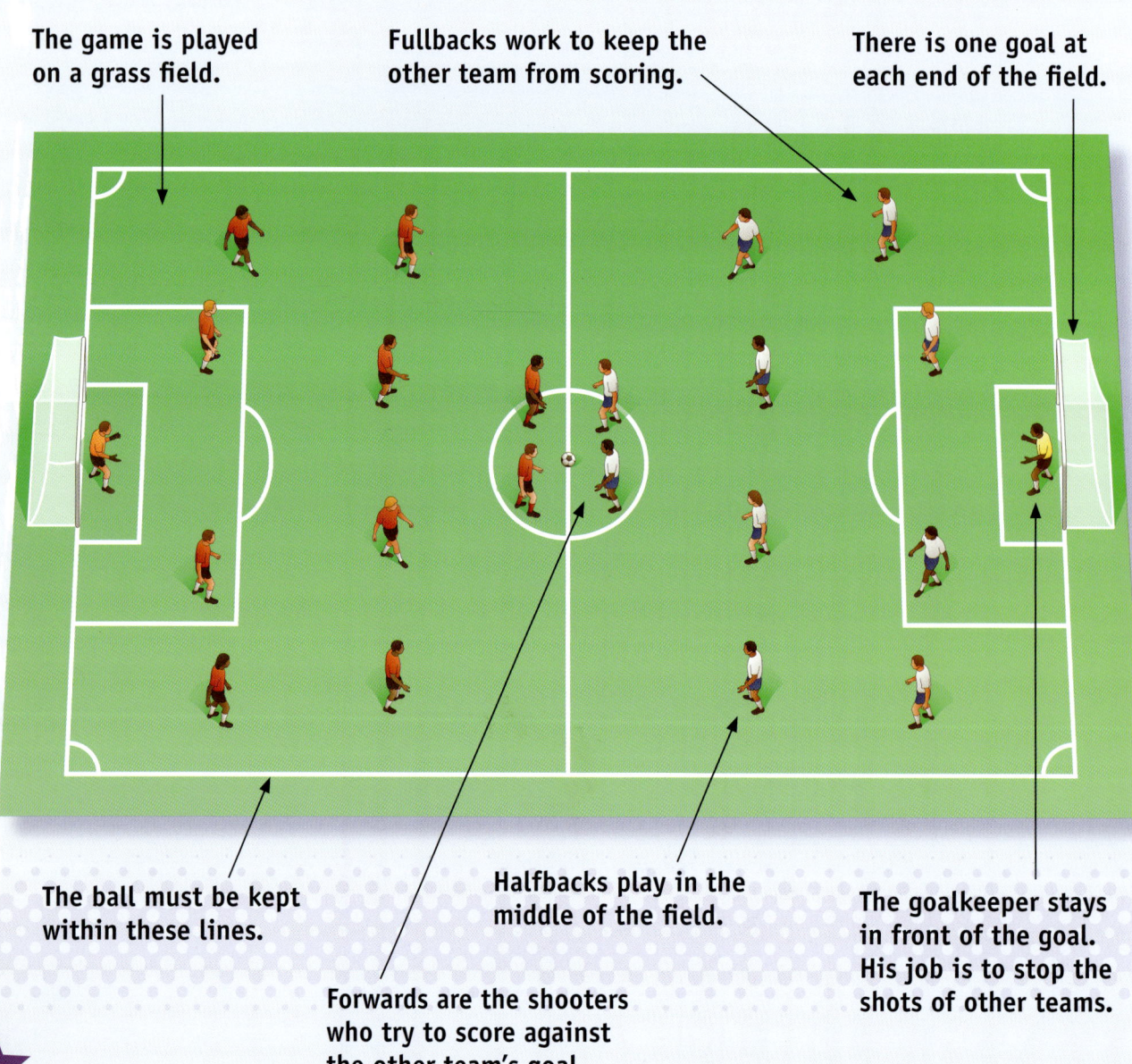

The game is played on a grass field.

Fullbacks work to keep the other team from scoring.

There is one goal at each end of the field.

The ball must be kept within these lines.

Halfbacks play in the middle of the field.

The goalkeeper stays in front of the goal. His job is to stop the shots of other teams.

Forwards are the shooters who try to score against the other team's goal.

Players also move the ball by hitting it with their heads. Players can't, however, touch the ball with their hands. Only a goalkeeper can use his or her hands to stop a shot.

Although the game is simple, it isn't easy. Scoring a goal can be a difficult task. Sometimes, one goal is all that a team needs to win a game.

A soccer team has 11 players on the field at a time.

The World Cup

The Americans and the English had come to Brazil to play in the World Cup, the **tournament** soccer fans love most! The World Cup is held every four years. Teams from different countries **compete** in a series of games. The winner becomes known as the best team in the world. People from the winning country are proud. They can brag about their team for four years straight!

Fans wave the American flag during the 2002 World Cup Finals.

Back in 1950, soccer fans were especially excited about the tournament. Due to **World War II**, there hadn't been a World Cup in 12 years. Fans had waited a long time!

About one quarter of all the people in the world watch the World Cup on TV—that's more than 1.5 billion people!

England's Team

Thirteen countries sent teams to the 1950 World Cup. One team stood tall above the rest—England.

The English team had lost only four times in its last 30 games. The team won games by huge scores—four, five, six goals or more.

Members of the English team train a month before the 1950 World Cup tournament.

Stanley Mortensen (left) during a soccer game in 1953

Players like Tom Finney and Stanley Mortensen were **masterful** scorers and wizards with the ball. England's goalkeeper, Bert Williams, was **exceptional**. He was like a brick wall blocking the English goal. Trying to get a ball past Williams was nearly impossible.

England was a truly mighty team! Most people thought the English would leave Brazil as champions.

England wasn't just home to soccer's best team; it was home to the sport itself. The modern game was invented there in 1863.

Soccer in America

The U.S. team, on the other hand, wasn't expected to do well. America wasn't known for having great soccer teams.

While the sport is popular in the United States today, it wasn't popular in 1950. Few schools had soccer teams. Many kids didn't play the game. Mainly **immigrants** and their children in big cities like St. Louis, New York, and Philadelphia played soccer.

Many children in St. Louis in the 1940s and 1950s played on soccer teams.

The immigrant families had come from countries such as Italy, Portugal, Haiti (HAY-tee), and Germany—places where soccer was loved. Many immigrants brought their excitement for the game with them when they came to the United States. They then taught their children how to play.

A boy's soccer game today

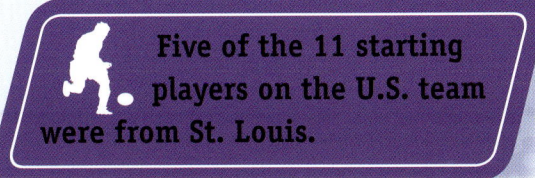

Five of the 11 starting players on the U.S. team were from St. Louis.

America's Team

Some of the U.S players were immigrants. None were full-time **professional** soccer players. In 1950, soccer wasn't like baseball or football. You couldn't earn a living playing it.

Forward Joe Gaetjens (GAYT-jenz) had come from Haiti to go to college in New York. To support himself, he washed dishes in a restaurant.

The Rimet Cup (above) was once the highest trophy given in the world of soccer. It was stolen shortly after it was awarded to Brazil in 1970. Today, World Cup Champions receive the FIFA World Cup trophy.

Fullback Harry Keough (KEE-oh) was a mailman. Midfielder Walter Bahr was a high school teacher. Goalkeeper Frank Borghi (BOR-gee) drove a **hearse** for a funeral parlor.

No one expected much from the U.S. team, but the players didn't care. They were going to Brazil. They were going to do their best.

A poster from the 1950 World Cup tournament

After the 1950 World Cup, the Americans didn't play in the finals again for 40 years! The U.S. team failed to **qualify** each time.

Brazil

The first team the Americans played was Spain. They lost the game. They didn't play badly. They didn't lose by a lot. Yet, they would have to play much better to do well in their second game.

The 1950 World Cup drew the biggest crowd ever for a soccer game—199,854. A total of 1,377,000 people attended the tournament.

The captains of the English and U.S. teams exchange souvenirs before the game.

Next up were the "Kings of Soccer," the powerful English team. On game day, the Brazilian fans filed into the stadium. Some fans were **rooting** for the Americans. If the Americans could knock out England, things would be easier for the Brazilian team to win.

Other fans just hoped to see a good game. Could the *Pobres Americanos*—poor Americans—even keep the score close?

The Big Game

The game began. Quickly, the English showed why they were considered the best. They made perfect passes. They faked out the Americans, dazzling them with tricky moves. They drove the ball swiftly across the field.

Crack! An English forward sent the ball flying in front of the American goal. Another English player caught the ball with his foot. He took aim and shot.

U.S. player Harry Keough (in the white shirt) goes up against Stanley Mortensen.

The ball sped toward the net. Frank Borghi, the American goalkeeper, tried to reach it. He couldn't!

Kerrang! The shot hit the post at the side of the net. The ball bounced harmlessly away. The Americans had gotten lucky!

Frank Borghi makes a save.

Before the 1950 World Cup game, the American coach had told reporters, "We don't have a chance."

Hanging Tough

As the first half continued, England kept up the attack. They kicked shot after shot at the American goal. Yet somehow, England didn't score. Time and again, Borghi **deflected** tough shots, leaping into the air or diving onto the ground.

The Americans barely had control of the ball. Whenever they got the ball, the English players stole it away.

Once again, Frank Borghi stops the English team from scoring.

Harry Keough "heads" the ball.

Still, the U.S. players refused to give up. They never stopped **hustling**. They ran for every ball. They challenged every play.

The Brazilian crowd, rooting for the **underdogs**, cheered the U.S. team on. The *Pobres Americanos* were making it a game!

> Soccer wasn't even Borghi's favorite sport. He loved baseball more. He had even played for the St. Louis Cardinals' minor league teams.

Heads Up!

When Walter Bahr kicked a ball toward England's goal, the crowd cheered wildly. They cheered as the ball sailed through the air. They cheered the American effort, though Bert Williams, the English goalkeeper, would surely stop it.

A SHOT HEARD AROUND THE WORLD

English Goalie Williams scrambles to catch the ball before it goes over goal line to register the world's soccer major upset. Joe Gaetjens of New York, not in picture, headed and deflected a shot by Walter Bahr of Philadelphia, past the surprised keeper.

A newspaper carried a photo of the winning shot

The U.S. team scores.

Williams moved to grab the ball, following it with his eyes. Joe Gaetjens followed the ball, too. He dove through the air. Somehow, he struck the ball with his head, changing its path ever so slightly.

The ball flew into the net, just out of the goalkeeper's reach. Goal! The Americans had scored! The stadium shook with the crowd's roar.

> A soccer game has two 45-minute halves. The Americans scored with eight minutes left in the first half.

Holding the Lead

There were still 53 minutes left in the game. Could the Americans keep their lead? The English kept firing away at the U.S. goal. Some shots went over the net. Some hit the posts. Frank Borghi blocked others.

The clock ticked down. England's players became more worried. The crowd's chanting grew louder and louder. The fans loved this American team that was struggling so hard to hold on.

Joe Gaetjens scored the most important goal in U.S. soccer history.

Finally, the whistle blew. The game was over! The score was England 0, U.S. 1. The Americans had won! Brazilian fans ran onto the field. They **hoisted** the Americans high into the air. They carried the players on their shoulders.

U.S. goalkeeper Frank Borghi rides on the shoulders of the fans.

Between 1949 and 1950, the American team's record before the World Cup Tournament was 1 win, 1 tie, and 4 losses.

The Little Team That Could

After the game against England, the Americans played Chile. They lost the game and didn't go on to win the World Cup. They didn't return home as heroes, either. In 1950, soccer just wasn't big news in America. In the years since, however, an **appreciation** has grown for the "little team that could."

Some members of the 1950 U.S. soccer team (left: Frank Borghi, John Souza, Walter Bahr, and Harry Keough) reunite in 2004.

An exhibit at the National Soccer Hall of Fame in Oneonta, NY, displays items from the 1950 game.

No one thought this victory was possible—not the fans, not the coach, not even the players. "In our wildest dreams we didn't think we'd ever win," said Harry Keough.

Yet, by refusing to back down from a challenge, and giving the game their all, they did win. The U.S. team created magic and pulled off the greatest upset in soccer history.

In 1976, all 11 of the starting players of the 1950 U.S. World Cup team were voted into the National Soccer Hall of Fame.

Just the Facts

More About the World Cup

★ **Who Won?**—Both the United States and England were eliminated from the 1950 tournament in the opening round. The team that took the World Cup title was Uruguay. They beat Brazil in the final game by a score of 2–1.

★ **Amazing Brazil**—Brazil is the most successful team in World Cup history. They've won the title five times and came in second twice.

★ **Counting Countries**—Today, over 150 countries play qualifying matches to get into the World Cup tournament. Only 32 teams make it.

★ **What About the Women?**—The men's World Cup began in 1930. Women didn't get their own tournament until 1991. Female American players have shown much more talent than the men. U.S. men's teams have never won the title. U.S. women have won it twice, in 1991 and 1999.

U.S. Women's Soccer team star Mia Hamm takes a shot on goal.

History of the World Cup (Final Games)

YEAR	FIRST PLACE	SECOND PLACE	SCORE
1930	Uruguay	Argentina	4–2
1934	Italy	Czechoslovakia	2–1
1938	Italy	Hungary	4–2
1950	Uruguay	Brazil	2–1
1954	West Germany	Hungary	3–2
1958	Brazil	Sweden	5–2
1962	Brazil	Czechoslovakia	3–1
1966	England	West Germany	4–2
1970	Brazil	Italy	4–1
1974	West Germany	The Netherlands	2–1
1978	Argentina	The Netherlands	3–1
1982	Italy	West Germany	3–1
1986	Argentina	West Germany	3–2
1990	West Germany	Argentina	1–0
1994	Brazil	Italy	0–0*
1998	France	Brazil	3–0
2002	Brazil	Germany	2–0

Won on penalty kicks.

Glossary

appreciation (uh-PREE-shee-*ay*-shun) enjoyment or thankfulness

compete (kuhm-PEET) to try as hard as possible in order to win

deflected (di-FLEKT-ed) caused to go in a different direction

exceptional (ek-SEP-shuh-nuhl) outstanding; unusually great

goal (GOHL) the rectangular net at each end of a soccer field; players try to kick the ball into this net in order to score

hearse (HURSS) a car that takes a coffin to the burial site

hoisted (HOIS-tid) lifted

hustling (HUHSS-uhl-ing) working fast and hard, giving extra effort

immigrants (IM-uh-gruhntz) people who come from one country to live permanently in a new one

masterful (MASS-tur-ful) extremely talented

professional (pruh-FESH-uh-nuhl) getting paid to do something rather than just doing it for fun

qualify (KWAHL-uh-fye) earn entry into an event by performing well

rooting (ROOT-ing) cheering

stadium (STAY-dee-uhm) a large building where events such as sports matches are held

tournament (TUR-nuh-muhnt) a series of games or contests that result in one player or team being chosen as champion

underdogs (UHN-dur-*dawgs*) athletes or teams that are not expected to win

World War II (WURLD WOR TOO) a world-wide conflict that involved many countries from 1939 to 1945

Bibliography

Douglas, Geoffrey. *The Game of Their Lives: The Untold Story of the World Cup's Biggest Upset.* New York: HarperCollins (2005).

Lewis, Michael. *"Miracle on Grass." Soccer Digest,* Aug./Sep. 2000, 23 (3), p. 12.

The International Federation for Association Football Web site. (www.fifa.com)

The National Soccer Hall of Fame. (www.soccerhall.org)

Read More

Crisfield, Deborah W. *The Everything Kids' Soccer Book.* Avon, MA: Sagebrush (2002).

Hornby, Hugh. *Soccer.* New York: DK Children (2005).

Howard, Dale E. *Soccer Around the World (World Cup Soccer).* New York: Children's Press (1994).

Kennedy, Mike. *Soccer.* New York: Children's Press (2002).

Learn More Online

Visit these Web sites to learn more about the sport of soccer and the World Cup:

library.thinkquest.org/29353

library.thinkquest.org/3903/

www.soccerhall.org/KidsZone_Index.htm

www.ussoccer.com

Index

Bahr, Walter 5, 15, 22, 26
Borghi, Frank 15, 19, 20–21, 24–25, 26
Brazil 8–9, 11, 15, 16–17, 21, 25, 28–29

Chile 26

dribble 6

England 4–5, 8–9, 10–11, 17, 18, 20, 22, 24, 26, 28

football 5
forwards 6, 18
fullbacks 6, 15

Gaetjens, Joe 14, 23, 24
Germany 13, 29
goal 5, 6–7, 10–11, 18, 20, 22–23, 24
goalkeeper 6–7, 11, 15, 19, 22–23, 25

Haiti 13, 14
halfbacks 6

immigrants 12–13, 14
invention of soccer 11
Italy 13, 29

Keough, Harry 15, 18, 21, 26–27
"Kings of Soccer" 5, 17

map 9
Mortensen, Stanley 11, 18

National Soccer Hall of Fame 27
net 6, 19, 24
New York 12, 14

Philadelphia 12
Pobres Americanos 17, 21
Portugal 13
professional soccer players 14

Spain 16
St. Louis 12–13, 21

Uruguay 28–29

Williams, Bert 11, 22–23
World Cup 4, 8–9, 10, 14–15, 16, 19, 25, 26–27, 28–29
World War II 9

About the Author

Michael Sandler lives in Brooklyn, New York. He has written numerous books on sports for children and young adults. His two children, Laszlo and Asha, are not quite old enough to read them yet.